OUTCRY OF LOVE

Pharos Books

ISBN: 978-93-55461-38-4
eISBN: 978-93-55461-46-9

©Publisher

Publisher: Pharos Books (P) Ltd.
Plot No.-55, Main Mother Dairy Road
Pandav Nagar, East Delhi-110092
Phone: 011-40395855, +14049995474
WhatsApp: +91 8368220032
E-mail: sales@pharosbooks.in
Website: www.pharosbooks.in
First Edition: 2022

Printed By: Sushma Book Binding House, Okhla
Industrial Area, Phase II, New Delhi-11002

OUTCRY OF LOVE
Sakis Tsilikis

Contents

CAST:

PART 1

DANAE A. (ACTOR) (the same person for all four roles of Danae)

DANAE B

DANAE C

DANAE D

SOCRATES (WRITER)

ARTEMIS (DIVA SINGER)

ALEXANDER (DIRECTOR)

ALKIS (STUDENT)

PART 2

1. MISS UTOPIA (SOMETHING LIKE A SURREAL TEACHER)

2. PARASKEVI (BIOLOGIST)

3. CONSTANTINE (CIVIL ENGINEER)

4. LOUKIANOS (ARCHITECT)

5. FOTEINI (PSYCHOLOGIST)

6. DIMITRIS (STUDENT)

7. EFI (STUDENT)

8. SOUZANA (FROM SWEDEN)

9. ART DIRECTOR

NOTES FROM THE AUTHOR

Music by composer **Sakis Tsilikis**.

SEASON OF MOURNING

SOCRATES: What are you doing here Danae?

DANAE: My car broke down and I'm waiting for the bus.

SOCRATES: Come on, I'll take you. Am I not your car God and more? Come on, let's go.

DANAE: How are you, you beast!?

SOCRATES: Beast! you can talk!.....It's been ten days since I last saw you..

DANAE: Oh baby! I've been busy, classes, jobs, I've been snowed-under.... And I know we were supposed to go out today, but I got called for TV rehearsal and I have to stay in and prepare.

SOCRATES: I think you are lying again, and this is all hot air and excuses, I can't take it anymore. You better listen to me. Your behaviour makes you look guilty. This makes me suspect that you have been lying for the past three months (pause). I am not accusing you, but I think you need to wake up so you can start realising certain things about your life...

DANAE: What do you mean? I don't understand your tone!....

SOCRATES: If you do this program on TV, you can hang me naked from the moon and call my muses to sing out of tune.... (Like the myth where Thamyris lost and so the muses hung him.)

No TV serial will happen sweetheart because nothing is done these days if you don't offer something else.... No job is just about the job. This is the pretext....

The media tycoons, that make no money, find a way to take advantage of the government and "get" the money in any case....

They just want money, and don't give a dam about anything else. That's why they only use established artists. They'd never spend a penny on an unknown like you.

Those who think they are great directors, but who are asexual and talentless are trapped within a microcosm are trying to make up stories to a young, budding star like you, who thinks she will save the world and the arts, when she can't even manage her "talent", or even her own body....

From this negative behavior of yours monsters are born. Your deficient behavior is stupid. If you have a son or a daughter, they will be abnormal. Not that I have a problem with abnormality, but you with your behavior even a rebellious poet like me will be turned into a plant.

DANAE: You're really having a go at me!....

SOCRATES: I'm the only one telling you the truth. But of course you probably think the only reason I'm having a go at you is because we haven't been sleeping together lately...

Since you found this new boyfriend and you are full of excuses and lies... And who is this new boyfriend?

A yuppie-pig, that's come across a goddess like you out of nowhere and does not know how to be with you...

Doesn't it scare you that he wants to make you a generic housewife? He doesn't know what he's got coming. What attracted you to someone like this? How can you be an authentic artist?

If you really were a free artist you wouldn't even spit on him let alone be with him... Your fear and your ego makes you be with him.

Screw this, you're busting my balls. Why are you doing it?

Instead of focusing on your career, you waste your time on this nobody wanker.... (Mimics her) "I don't have time.. I don't have time", but if you were to manage time correctly you could be creative and in turn be happy.

Self-awareness is at least about knowing why you are sleeping with who you're sleeping with. When I held your clitoral orgasm on my tongue all the heavens celebrated with us....

If there is no eroticism, erection, revolution, ideology and freedom in love then it does not exist.

DANAE: Okay, it's true, but I loved you even if it sounds strange. I wanted to be close to you and to spend my nights with you because that gave me the greatest sense of security.

SOCRATES: That's exactly what I didn't want. When you wake up with someone morning after morning, it becomes a trap, a routine and then you end up splitting up... I suppose you'll tell me we've broken up anyway, but for different reasons...

I feel gutted. This was the last thing I wanted. It would have been fine if you told me you would sleep with him in advance, instead of doing it in secret and telling me later. It doesn't matter. You can stay the way you are: fearful and with that boyfriend... and I'll move on with a new love. I'll be fine.

Remember?

What was written on my wall: 'The best thing in the world is a woman, or... another woman' ...but now that seems ironic, but may be for my own good. It's likely I will never overcome mourning love. This grief is universal, and has and always will happen.

No couple ever lasts, so it should be understood love is mortal, and then our consciousness awakes like lightning.

One needs emotional intelligence. Whether you have meaningless sex or romantic love making, in the end you will sink into abyss and unbearable disappointment.

DANAE: I know. I might spend my life depressed. I want to re-live glorious moments of our erotic past.

SOCRATES: Unfortunately eroticism is lived once, and you rushed, and I fear we cannot escape this contemporary illness...

Our friends throw themselves into depression, like a strange rain over them and eventually we all experience this illness...

Depression, while we were in love, were non-existent, now your recklessness has brought us to the same point.

The modern grief of love

Just so that we don't forget...

SOCRATES: Tell me, does he fuck well?

10

DANAE: Don't.....

SOCRATES: I am waiting for an answer.......

DANAE: Yes....

SOCRATES: Is he better than me....

DANAE: Different.....

SOCRATES: What does that means?

DANAE: Now whatever happened happened... Don't overdo it, calm down....

SOCRATES: So you are trying to be a "Madonna" to feel less guilty. How do you feel?

DANAE: Guilty.

SOCRATES: So you're telling me, you're sleeping with him every night and you're coming! Yesterday for example what happened?

DANAE: Why are you doing this?

SOCRATES: Because I want to know and understand so I can have closure...

DANAE: Yes, I came...

SOCRATES: How many times?

DANAE: Two, at first he went down on me and then he fucked me from behind. Why is sex so important to men?

SOCRATES: It is as important for men as it is for women. Ever since the time of Adam man is castrated. Do you toss him off sometimes?

DANAE: We do what the entire world does when making love.

SOCRATES: Do you like him coming in your face?

DANAE: A lot.

SOCRATES: How does it taste?

DANAE: As it tastes with you...

SOCRATES: You're a scared hooker, fearful, and have insincere feelings and everything's messed up in you. I want you to make a fresh start based on truth and your real needs. I'm your truth and the meaning of your life. At the stage you're at, you should dedicate yourself to your goals, your work and then you should choose the person instead of them choosing you. A friend once called me a carnivore! Now I think I'm gentler and wiser.

Women have liposuction, puncturing their bellies, irons put in their stomachs, hair removal. They go through all the torture of the world for eroticism and when that moment comes instead of consenting, they refuse. And then they won't let you do them from behind, saying it hurts. Suddenly pain is an issue! Don't fall into the trap of backward Christian morality...

DANAE: You are right, I don't disagree. But (and maybe you didn't realise it) you treated me like a mere object of pleasure instead of a woman and lover. Sometimes you made me feel like an animal of nature, whose scent enticed your desires, and that was all.

SOCRATES: I didn't expect to hear this, for you to obliterate my love and affection after so many years. You make me feel like "beast" from Beauty and the Beast, the Valerian Borovzik film, but even in the film the rape of the girl by the beast is a crowning moment in the anthology of world cinema.... Even if we look as a film paradox, this grotesque aesthetic by the director moved us forward. Don't try to justify the unjustifiable darling, that so many have done in life and in art. When a third person becomes involved this always brings turmoil and imbalance.

Since we're on the topic of film, the taking of the girl (Ntogkvil) an entire village was transformed and all the good, religious folk became the monster. How would a young, innocent girl like you face that kind of adversity? Refusal takes consciousness and courage to be implemented.

The new generation think they refuse dishonest, immoral issues, but in reality they nod their heads. I'll anticipate your return when your memories of me conquer you. Because you will understand what we were about and how every new man brings you misery. Besides, I will confide my guilt.

When I shaped you with my personality I knew that once you acquire my aestheticism and culture you'd be mine forever. Yesterday I found out that you told our friends that we've broken up.

They were shocked, and they took your side because they thought I was in the wrong.

That's what you told them. Did you tell them what you did to me and how you killed my confidence? You never listen to me, I am crying for help....

DANAE: How dare you shout? You sleep with whoever you like!

SOCRATES: You never understood me, you never supported me really.

DANAE: What about me? The only thing I ever wanted from you was for you to respect my art...

SOCRATES: Do you know how exhausting it is to support someone you don't believe in?

DANAE: I am not talking to you anymore. You consider my art rubbish. You're such an asshole...

SOCRATES: How dare you? Do we have to continue believing a talent myth, an illusion, a fantasy?

DANAE: Fuck off asshole, fuck off....

SOCRATES: You are a fucking unauthentic artist, look at what you've done to me. I could kill you, I could kill you....

DANAE: Go on then....

(They look at each other and he kisses her passionately. Equally excited, she undoes his trousers.)

DANAE and SOCRATES: I adore you!.....

THE SEASON OF YES

ARTEMIS: Are you not a good friend of mine DANAE, or am I wrong?

DANAE B': No, you aren't wrong. I've been staring at your photo for ages and I'm still at this bus stop.

ARTEMIS: You're looking good, and now you're an actress, I've seen you in the papers...I can see you're going for it.

DANAE B': You say it with so much admiration... and what should I say about your bright career...

ARTEMIS: Well, it's no big deal, all part of the game, it wasn't easy getting here.... You need to sell something of yourself to get somewhere, but what scares me the most is now I am owned. I've come to belong to an establishment; in what's called "cultural imperialism". Hmm and so I have a say in it too (pause). What's your news?

DANAE B': Nothing special. I'm also giving my all to my career and I encounter difficulties too.

However, when it gets knocked down, I have something to lean on, I turn to our childhood memories. I look back not out of nostalgia but to bring back the emotion of innocence, and the love I had for you ... Do you think of me ever..?

ARTEMIS: Of course, we all go back to our childhood....

DANAE B': I loved you a lot and now I think of it I feel complete, without any sense of guilt, and anyway what is guilt? We had the best memories as children and lived in an age of innocence. When our thoughts are pure then there is nothing sordid. Most people can't stand pure thinking....

ARTEMIS: It's sometimes good to be one step ahead of reality.

DANAE B': Your body is still as it was! And I still know your scent.... Remember how well we got on? I always go back to you. When things get tough and men don't understand, what do they understand, even when they're old they'll still love their mothers....

Their lives are stolen by their careers, and when they do love, they become possessive and act like assholes: "where did you go?", "what did you do?", "who are you checking out now"? My darlings.. What a misery it must be to be a man after all! ....

We must sound like "little lesbians" but we aren't. We are more than a gender and a libido. I love the phallus and you, as I remember you like God... So in the end men and women alike all love the phallus. No, we are not at risk of becoming lesbians. We have always been "main stream" in our love lives. Our innocence obliterated every obstinate idiot and kept our love holy. My heart beats as strongly now as it did then on the train, do you remember?

ARTEMIS: I remember it like it's in the present........

DANAE B': I live and live the eternal now, because that's all that counts. Back then "yes" was innocent and emotional, now everything is "no", nothing.....

Is there life without rhythm? What would life be without that incredible rhythm? Like a thousand drummers joined us in reaching our climax in the train toilet.

We were travelling to Athens and at Tempi the Temple of Olympian Gods joined us in our rhythm of crescendo... tack-tack the sound of the train, tick-tack the sound of our hearts, that beat at an even faster pace than the train's......

ARTEMIS: You will always be able to touch me with that same innocence.

DANAE B': I hope to see you more and catch up ... I'd love that, but I don't know how realistic that'll be considering how busy you are.. with your love-life and your fans....

Maybe I also get caught up in everything and am busy too, so I don't know if we'll be able to meet more often....

Let's leave it to chance and things will work themselves out.....

ARTEMIS: I really want to keep in touch though..... I think we lost touch abruptly, or am I mistaken?

DANAE B': You're right, we did split up abruptly... and that left me torn.

My nightmare was that other person..

Remember when you asked me: Are you not afraid, wondering around Omonia square at three in the morning with all the drug-addicts? And I told you I feel safer? That was because I didn't tell you what was happening at home with my brother..

He raped me ever since childhood. As I got older, he got scared that I would go to the police and became worse. He was threatening and tormenting me.

When the nightmare of rape is also incest, and from an immediate family member, you are pushed to the edge, you struggle to survive, somewhere between schizophrenia and suicide.

I could have been calmer in overcoming this tragic experience. What was unbearable was the violent behaviour of my brother that went from predatory to fear of being caught.

A third person, a third occurrence, decisively eradicated the age of innocence that we had then and we live in a nightmare present and the future is unpredictable and hard.

I don't believe in happiness that lasts ... I believe in happy moments. Every time I tried to catch happiness something always changed....

Something ended that started something new. Only before death will I be able to look back over my life and say if I was happy.

My mind, body and heart was left in the streets of Nafplion as if forgotten there....

Often it's good to remember! But at other times it's best to forget. My way of forgetting was to leave my mind and body behind in Nafplion.

Now if we fall in love again it may lack innocence... in this loveless time we will be called lesbians....

Not that I care what people say but the season of "yes" and innocence is over.

You never know.... when a time comes when security guards guard poets instead of banks... then maybe we'll be able to love again ....

Good night sweetheart, I adore you...! (Both)

THE SEASON OF NO

DANAE C': Alexander, when did you come to Athens? Why didn't you call me? What's new darling?

ALEXANDER: What's up baby? It seems to me that death will either separate us or unite us. I buried my father last week and all was well... I mean that this time there were no problems like when my mother died....

DANAE C': I don't believe it!

ALEXANDER: Believe it or not, that's the truth, we buried my father without a problem...

DANAE C': Are you trying to tell me that you've gone from rebel and poet to a religious yuppie?

ALEXANDER: Not really, but you know things aren't as they were... we don't have dictators and crap, and priests don't bother us as they did....

Religion goes hand in hand with right wing politics whose only interest is in accumulating wealth while the masses have less and less to live off....

Nowadays, the youth, even in anti-globalization, seem to have the feeling that their future is bleak.

They protest more to disconnect themselves from the situation rather than try to prevent it....

And governments, past as well as present, tell the youth that resist "you are useless, and use only words and practice revolutionary gymnastics, and we don't listen"... So in that respect nothing has changed....

DANAE C': Ok Alexander, today's youth and my generation are decent and idealist. Regardless of whether or not there have been exceptions... even the university that stole money in the vilest way, belong to past generations...

ALEXANDER: So the bitterness in my mouth for the dead end of -isms and whichever political revolution I turned it to a more stimulating and enjoyable 'position'... after all these years I'm calmer....

Now our revolutionary mood moves towards sex, because in these loveless times only sex harmonises us...

DANAE C': When did you return from Sweden? Did you make any films? Are you doing any Swedish television at the moment?

ALEXANDER: You don't need to pity Sweden's citizens. It is a country that's organised, and at least as far as the basics are concerned, takes care of its citizens. Not like our shithole over here.... You know, if you live abroad and come to Greece you think you've arrived in a third world country, here as a state and as a society we are bullshit and it's a shame........

DANAE C': Darling, after all these years I still go back to that week we were together and it has marked me forever... back then I was young and I didn't know much, but now that I remember it... I remember and admire you and I remember and I love you - and even if I've realised it late, how right you were to resist ....

ALEXANDER: Yes, the time was such... that we learned to say "no" to the dictators and to every mindless state because "no" wasn't just an act then it was the act.

The quest for democracy and for truth is a timeless necessity. For a fascist regime, a mentality may exist but at some point in the weight of democracy and truth it will collapse.

Just as truth is in theatre or in life, the quest is for the truth.

We experience daily life with the painful memory of an open wound. Loss is hell. Without lasting love and dialogue you reach your limits. You experience misery through your own body in real time...

As soon as you recognise happiness it is gone. Eventually happiness is nothing more than a game of memories with shadows.

Creation takes time, patience and perseverance while disaster takes moments.

In the end time is a tyrant God.

The unfulfilled journey of life.

Who is going to govern our tomorrow?

What is the truth?

DANAE C': Alexander, I am trying to live the illusion through a vehicle within art. Maybe creation

is the essence of life, or it may be a lie... I am not bothered by lies, I'm not afraid of lies and I create my own world, without caring if that world is the truth...
ALEXANDER: Your thoughts scare me a little, and could even be dangerous. It might be redemptive as personal truth, but with the lie of dictatorship and fascist regimes imposed in time, humanity has paid with millions of deaths.

DANAE C': You beast, I was scared that they might not bury your mother Athena if you didn't pay them and especially if you didn't want to accept their Christian barbarism.

Even death needs to be financed in today's misery.

Young as I was then, I had my fears and my guilt. But now I realize that you resisted by saying a big "no" towards attitudes and ideologies that were keeping humanity back. I remember they had left your mother unburied for ten days and they were lost in their stupidity and their persistence. We made love on your mother's coffin and I almost had a seizure. But when you told me: 'ALEXANDER, don't be horrified baby, through death comes life and through love we will exorcise death...' Then I calmed down.

ALEXANDER: The carnal erotic spasm is a preparation of death's spasm, the harbinger brings us the end of life. In that case we have the requiem of despair.

Making love means I exist...

Love is almost a metaphysical ideology. Love and sex are lonely feelings ...endless loneliness, general tests of death which abolish gender and time....

A relationship can be present on an initial level as authoritarian violence, but can also have a charm such as the raw instincts of dictatorship...

A merciless exploitation of human frailty favours the superhuman will for power and for life...

DANAE C': I am fascinated and I love what you said... Then I was redeemed, became a woman forever and "human", then I realized and it didn't bother me that the child we were meant to have never came to be.... don't forget this... since you left me for a blonde Scandinavian... what I learned and I realised, is that the highest pleasure, is to be equal to God - since through the death of your dearly beloved lost one came new life, and the tomorrow. ..

ALEXANDER: It's necessary for us all to have spiritual decisiveness, so to be able to define the real truth of our lives and our society.... If such a situation is not incorporated in our political vision then there is no hope in restoring what we have lost, our human dignity....

DANAE C': Alexander, you are my timeless object of desire and my great love, after all you taught me that, music, poetry, and art is generally purple ... The blue of sky, which is calm and spirit, red of passion and struggle, thus true purple...

ALEXANDER: Yes darling, purple is not the colour of mourning. I think in the end that we should never mourn if we could accept the physical truth of necessity and not what religious ideologies dictate. We would always be happy and fearless....

DANAE C': Fear ....out of fear I agreed to marry someone that my parents imposed on me and I spoilt the wonderful relationship we had....

And I know that this was the reason you left for Sweden. But.... with your hands and teeth take my neck and remove this chain and let me lose myself in your embrace, desires that are pinned within my tongue....

These hands of yours see you and want to break the branches and the murmur inside your veins. I love you and will love you forever, but off you go now because if I could kill you I would wrap you in violets. Oh what a disaster, the fire in my head that's ignited... Oh what madness, I want you as a bed-mate and a dinner companion and to be with you every moment... Because you drag me and I follow, you tell me to come back to you and I do like grass swaying in the wind.... I gave up a man then, and his family to follow you... I want to sleep amidst your legs and guard your dreams...

My timeless secret is that we can no longer live together...

30

But you accompany me with your deep resounding silence forever....

Alexander, I'm not afraid anymore because...

I adore you! ....(Both)

THE SEASON OF YES AND MAYBE

ALKIS: What are doing here babe?

DANAE D': Can't you see? I've been waiting for an hour for the fucking bus and it still hasn't come…. and I have rehearsal and I won't make it…….

ALKIS: In that case I'll take you…

DANAE D': I had the impression that you were upset with me, or was I wrong?

ALKIS: Not really….

DANAE D': Alki, I played a very honest game with you, however, measuring honesty by my morality, my aesthetics and not others…

After all, everyone knew this game and don't tell me it's not so, even if we never discussed it all three of us were accomplices.

You knew and you came every morning to hide yourself in my arms and would then flee with sadness in your eyes….

Because you knew your brother would come soon. You never thought to stop caring about me because you knew how much I loved you both with the same intensity.

For me it was the same person all in one. I put you both on scales to see which of you I loved more, and the scale was equally balanced.

Really, who teaches us to love only one person? Who determines the number one, and not two or three? Someone who has a reason or an interest of course.

I lived countless nights listening to my soul, playing with my thoughts, not able to choose one of you.....

Amongst you the youngest, the rebel and therefore powerful aphrodisiac, and Pericles the elder one, calmest, and more secure in what he did... For me one completed the other, one was part of the other....

If your mother had found out she would certainly say the obvious:

"Slut, whore, e.t.c." I don't want to judge your mother but if she were to learn this is what she would say...

But in my conscience, the love triangle is allowed, it might seem like a scandal but for me it works as it disorganizes urban order. It's the inverting of things, and rebellious...

A housewife and the family and the bourgeois morality can reward a woman who lives in the status quo circumstances, but in reality is a household prostitute.......

I would like my life to be independent, autonomous and creative and free self-determined.

I remember that film starring Simone Signoret, when she was going through the menopause, took the gun and shot her genitals as an eternal heroin of Greek tragedy.

When love ends, life ends....

Sometimes I feel like Hedda Gabbler in the tragedy of incompatibility, within the drama of individuality against the common measure imposed by the existing conservative ideology.

Hedda and every strong woman is not only a knot of neurosis and hysteria, but a tragedy of the wilderness of the soul, which begins the climbing of

34

a dream and faces the sad face of life. Settle or confront.

The end is not moral conclusion but the poetic suicide of dreams.

ALKIS: As a matter of fact, I didn't realized that, in this way, I admire you...

DANAE D': Alkis, people who are possessive are insecure and easily consider everything theirs...

But what is ours? What's "mine"? If it were not so mankind would be different.

This is not a theoretical scheme Alki, nor preaching, even if we say all this in the middle of the road. What difference does it make where we say it!

Misery and war is rooted in the idea of 'mine' and ownership. A 'mine' is an atomic bomb in the foundations of people's happiness.... and what is happiness and who has it ... shouldn't "mine" go fuck itself?

ALKIS: Could you speak to me simply, I like listening to you; The next words don't come easily to me... would you want us to be together forever?

DANAE D': To say "Together forever" or "Only together" will not change the world or us. As social animals we create bonds together as we share our feelings and complicity....

The need for communication is hidden in a smile. Because those who cry, laugh. Those who hurt do the same. Sooner or later, everyone will laugh as a sign that life goes on....

ALKIS: In the end what are the basic aspects of your character? I ask in an attempt to understand you better.

DANAE D': I'm trying to work it out.. I search myself but I don't want to find myself. By having the illusion of spaciousness, I do not want to be in confined in pre-determined spaces....

ALKIS: Fine! Tell me your faults, where are you vulnerable?

DANAE D': I want to have greed for life! To lack discipline. To exaggerate. To be here and now I want it all. To not have fear of rejection. To not be pulled into empty time, and an empty future. And sometimes I feel sad for all the people I have known who are now gone and who I could have had a more meaningful relationship with....

ALKIS: I'm starting to understand... What are you most afraid of?

DANAE D': I'm afraid that one day I will fear nothing, which means I'll be dead. Life is never as beautiful, or as ugly as we think ... but it is all we have....

What's sudden scares me. What's slow pushes me away. To be honest I would prefer not to die. I will always be in a state of consciousness and readiness. Live for life Alki, drink its juices, and exceed it, perhaps the only reason to live is life itself.

Will you take me to the rehearsal babe?

ALKIS: Let's go. I want to speed and clear my mind.

I adore you! (Both)

THE SOLUTION OF DRAMA

WE LEARNED FROM THE PRESS THAT ALKIS AND DANAE D' CRASHED INTO A COLUMN.

ALKIS WAS KILLED.

BUT DANAE D' AFTER THE MIRACULOUS EFFORTS FROM THE DOCTORS AND ESPECIALLY HER GOOD MEMORIES WHICH OPERATE AS REDEEMER MAGICALLY, LIVED.

CONCLUSION

LIFE IS HOT

LIFE IS COLD

BUT NOT LUKEWARM

YES TO ALL

THE HONEYMOON

"GUILTY – TRUTH"

UTOPIA: Is there anyone here who is called Messiah, Jesus, or The Holy Spirit?

Fuck off then everybody. My soul is sickened by you.

I confess that your apathy and masochism is beyond any limit.

It's been ages and I haven't heard any voice of protest! If you behave better, Miss Utopia may teach you some sexology.

Why not sex... (angrily) where do you think you are? Here I expect a little respect.

I am the boss hereeeeee, you want to see the pussy of Miss Utopia, don't you?

Fuck off, you filthy children.

Miss utopia is your second mother.

She wants to help you graduate from primary school after you've been to university and secondary school.

Here we'll do it in reverse. We will be in reverse of the universe....

Eventually you will become asshole doctors, asshole lawyers, asshole architects and asshole businessmen, as it is in Brassens' song.

According to my thinking and logic, people are born old and then age younger into infants. As a child at least you die without any guilt or remorse and so are closer to truth and innocence.

When you age and have sinned who will forgive you!.....

So it's much better to be born old and then die as children in eternal innocence! .....

Who are you?

FOTINI: I am Fotini, mrs, miss! I am the most miserable of all because I have been cheated on all my life.....

UTOPIA: Who are you, my child?

LOUKIANOS: Loukianos, miss Utopi(a), I am an architect.

UTOPIA: You sweetheart?

PARASKEUI: I am Paraskeui, miss. I am a Biologist.

UTOPIA: And you, my child?

CONSTANTINE: Civil engineer miss, Constantine who evolved into a 'Greekified', crazy entrepreneur.....

Also, Miss Utopia, I was able to double the money my father-in-law gave me.

UTOPIA: Tell me all about you Loukiane......

LOUKIANOS: Me, miss, I was a very good pupil at school, then an excellent student at university and emotionally attached to Paraskeui and then we decided to get married, we went on a honey moon to an island.... with two of our friends Constantinos and Fotini.....

UTOPIA: Come on Constantinos tell us all about your crimes and your truths.....

CONSTANTINE: Me? Miss, I grew up in complete poverty and when I got back from Germany where I had studied I got married to Fotini, in all honesty for her money..... And so went on our honey moon on an island with Paraskeui and Loukiano.........

UTOPIA: So you were two married couples in the same place at the same time... which for the two of you proved to be the right place and time, but for the other two, an absolutely devastating moment in time...

I therefore want you all to confess your guilt so we can understand what happened so we can tell if you were innocent in your stupidity, or guilty with conscience...

PARASKEUI: Me my Mrs Miss, when I was little I was in love with Constantinos, but my parents, society, and fate brought me to marry Loukianos .....

There on the island, even though it was our honey moon month, I couldn't stand it. I wanted Constantinos like crazy hell because he's so beautiful... he aroused all my senses....

My greatest rapture was after having sex with my husband, sending messages to Constantinos.... And writing "I adore you".... That was when I really climaxed, and felt like a woman...

His presence turned me upside down and he became a forbidden fruit to me, he was exciting my entire hormonal system to its core.

Love making with him is like a lightning rod because it makes us immortal. I never felt guilty because I knew he was the only man for me.

Every woman has a different level of prostitute within her, but my thoughts and later relationship, made me take off without any sense of guilt ... However, when we later had a family of two children, I remained completely loyal.

LOUKIANOS: I, Miss Utopia, was in love with Paraskeui ever since I was a child and so thought I should marry her, even if I toyed round with other girls..... Paraskeui gave me steadiness and so was worth staying with all my life....

Life of course is unpredictable and writes its own scenario.

When I understood that my wife's relationship with Constantinos was fixed, I wanted to kill myself. My bitterness made me sleep with men in my attempt to escape this torturous dependence that reduced me as a man, as a scientist and as a social figure to nothing....

So years later, when I decided to live the orthodox way again, life again wrote its own script, and set a path for new injury.

It turned out the woman I married from Sweden was sleeping with the brother of my ex-wife, and so from that fucking family I have only ever been defeated and destroyed....

STUDENT DIMITRIS: I to start with was unsuspicious, for two reasons. Firstly the drugs which I got messed up in without realizing it, and second the sudden attraction to men.....

It doesn't take much with drugs. At first it was curiosity, then habit, and finally addiction. And as if that were not enough, I began to deal to afford my hit. Something negative came between my girlfriend and I that ended the relationship.

And when I went to prison, drowning and losing my mind, he came... In the beginning I needed him desperately almost dependently. His presence brought me intrigue. I saw that he was my only way out to freedom.... Without realizing it, I began to be attracted to him.

Something twisted inside me and I found myself in love with him and dependant on him. Who?!! I, that had only ever loved women! My relationship with Loukianos didn't last, but it marked me forever.....

STUDENT EFI: My own shock was huge and powerful. I found myself in despair. First the loss of my loved one from this damned illness, the drugs; fuck the drug dealers and the government that does nothing....

Initially I lost Dimitri, who was weak physically and mentally and could no longer love me. And then I lost him completely.

Dimitri was in the arms of a man. And it was then that I started hating men, women, and gay people, people in general. I hated myself, others, and found myself in a vacuum and conscience of deadlock, deadlock of memory, and particularly with no appetite and no vision for the future... all destroyed.

In the end we live in a parody of our own pursuit. We are all losers.

SUSANA: To be honest, I came to Greece and I was out of it. I opened a beauty salon; as this was what I was good at, and married Loukianos so as to live a family life as my parents taught me....

Just like Greek films where couples marry and live happily ever after....

However, I understood too late that films like life, start after the wedding day..... My husband Loukianos rapidly distanced himself from me in bed and also from home....

That's when Paraskevi's brother came into my life. He was cruel, violent and neurotic....

However, I started sleeping with him because my wounds in Greece became increasingly large and I was trying to keep myself together.... But when the storm ended I felt empty....

I move my loneliness to the province's completely black back....

Walking as a glorious monk, who contemplates the bright, young, brave men.... dressed with horns.......

CONSTANTINE: Ok Loukianos. I will not apologize for Paraskeui's brother who was fucking your wife. Neither will I accept that I took your ex-wife.

I operate as a predator, either with the money, or sex, in this way Paraskevi fell into my arms...

Maybe it's an invisible need where people exceed, against any logic.

Paraskevi came to me and I had no reason to refuse her. When things evolved she came to me perhaps because this was fate...

UTOPIA: Come on darling; tell us all about you.... you've been a mute.

FOTINI: No one's thought about me? You took my money, you took my youth and now I am raising your daughter in complete loneliness. Like a heroine of Greek tragedy.....

It's torturous raising a sick child alone as if damned destiny sent it. I raise your daughter amidst my loneliness and pride.

What pride and what life, where the only reason I live is to get revenge ... I'll have revenge over you with all the power of my soul in the hope that you will understand one day that you are nothing more than a macho pig. All I wanted was to be with you. I wanted it all with you. Later I cut our child into pieces and put her in the fridge, when you were the one I really wanted to shred.....

I was led into this act, because I left social norms, and became a crazy witch, one of those people we avert...

When you reach the deepest point of despair and are left with no choice. You have only one choice: revenge. A contemporary Medea? Medea by Euripides....

Whether contemporary pain, or timeless pain, the wound is always big and deep. I feel anger and pain and I feel like destroying you two arseholes right here and every other man in the world.....

Exactly like the "IPSILIS" by Euripides were in Limnos all the neglected women from their men have performed deceitful but just thoughts. They banished all the men from the island. Unfair, inequitable, awful, and "wonderful", but justified when men behave so cowardly..... A husband is a calm force, a great spirited God and a loving father who protects his child his whole life. You idiot, running after any skirt, where were you, when your child was in need with a fever?

UTOPIA: What do you have to say you creep?

CONSTANTINE: I understand your anger Fotini! Medea and Ipsipili, but it's in man's nature, like Odysseus, to search, to change places, and so why not women too....

It's not in man's nature to settle in one port and wait to die.... If you want to judge you can judge man's nature, and mankind, not me......

PARASKEVI: This is a human nature for everyone. Men and women can't live alone without man's caress and power.

How dull a man's society would be without women. Any one-dimensional society would be a misspelling. Both genders should coexist harmoniously.

.   UTOPIA: It sounds fine to me, go on Fotini!

FOTINI: I would agree with all of it if I had known, even for a while, love. From the genus of men I have felt only bitterness. Men and women are dominated by their phallus and the phallus emperor has suppressed us for centuries.... Even today a woman is forbidden to enter the altar of a church or Agios Oros (The holy mountain). How holy can a mountain be which prohibits the presence of women?

Which dark minds have such ideas and perpetuate them? All men and women that have such dull thoughts should be burned.

UTOPIA: Open your minds assholes and look at life beyond your phallus and genetelia. Love and be loved.

FOTINI: What is the value of all this in the face of death? It is important to know how to live so as to hold a stance against death.

The loss of our neighbour and every loss is unbearable. The only way to overcome loss is through love and love making.

Love and love making is timeless and endless. But I've never experienced its sweet scent only the horror of loneliness and distress. I've raised a child all alone.

(Utopia faints and falls.)

UTOPIA: My doctors have told me not to get distressed but with everything I've heard I have had a small blackout. However, I don't die as easily as you think. Miss Utopia does not die, she will always be at your side and will hear you, today all of you, the next year others, then your children and then your children's children... I will always be here as time passes, moreover is anyone perfect? Nobody.

ACTORS SHARING WORDS

1. Love is a matter of chemistry which is why the others treat us like toxic waste.

2. There are two kinds of people, those who want to stay and those who want to leave. Unfortunately those who get married later wonder why they get separated.

3. Women can fake an orgasm, but men fake entire relationships.

4. Women are labeled the opposite sex, because when you want to do something they want the opposite.

5. I like to go shopping when a relationship ends, to see if there is something nice in a shop window. And if there is when I am still attached then I'll separate anyway.

6. Women and men, battle between sexes and want different things. Women want men and men want women.

Only love will save us.

Utopia I love you!

Utopia we love you! (All together)

I love you! (All together)

FINALE

ART DIRECTOR

Come on guys, the programs and the costumes just arrived. Get dressed, we're doing the photo shoot soon. The rehearsal didn't go badly but it didn't all go as we agreed. I do not know if what we said was understood for the overthrow of "better to be born old than die young" innocent within our complete confusion.

What I am trying to do, is to open a window to get a glimmer of light in our lives.

We belong to the seekers.

Come and sing the last song then go and have a rest because tomorrow for the premiere you will need stamina and to be wide awake.

Moreover the president will be attending....

ONE
TWO
THREE
FOUR
LET'S GO!

SONG

FINALE